For Alexis. — A. R.
For my dad. — C. K.

Library of Congress Cataloging-in-Publication Data:

Names: Rex, Adam, author. | Keane, Claire, illustrator.
Title: Why? / written by Adam Rex ; illustrated by Claire Keane.
Description: San Francisco, California : Chronicle Books LLC, [2019] | Summary: Would-be supervillain Doctor X-Ray swoops into the mall, threatening destruction, only to be confronted by a little girl asking "why" to his every declaration, until finally he is forced to reveal, and understand, the root of his anger—and so departs in peace.
Identifiers: LCCN 2018033420 | ISBN 9781452168630 (alk. paper)
Subjects: LCSH: Supervillains—Juvenile fiction. | Bullying—Juvenile fiction. | Self-evaluation—Juvenile fiction. | Self-perception—Juvenile fiction. | Interpersonal communication—Juvenile fiction. | CYAC: Supervillains—Fiction. | Bullying—Fiction. | Self-perception—Fiction. Classification: LCC PZ7.R32865 Wh 2019 | DDC [E]—dc23 LC record available at https://lccn.loc.gov/2018033420

Manufactured in China.

Design by Jennifer Tolo Pierce.
Typeset in Air and Air Condensed.
The illustrations in this book were rendered digitally.

10 9 8 7 6 5 4 3 2

Chronicle Books LLC
680 Second Street
San Francisco, California 94107

Chronicle Books—we see things differently. Become part of our community at www.chroniclekids.com.

Written by **ADAM REX**

Illustrated by **CLAIRE KEANE**

chronicle books · san francisco

AT THE MALL...